GEORGE SHANNON

Oh, I Love!

Illustrated by CHERYL HARNESS

Bradbury Press / New York

10 9 8 7 6 5 4 3 2 1

Library of Congress Cataloging-in-Publication Data
Shannon, George. Oh, I love! Summary: A lullaby repeats the sounds made by a rooster, pig, chick, goose, lamb, and "my little baby" too.   1. Children's Poetry. American.   [1. Lullabies.   2. Animal sounds—Poetry.   3. American poetry]   I. Harness, Cheryl, ill. II. Title.
PS3569.H33503   1988   811'.54   87-15092
ISBN 0-02-782180-3

Oh, I Love! has grown as George Shannon's personal extension of the North American folk song most widely known as "My Little Rooster" or "The Barnyard Song." As a cumulative song, it can include as many kinds of animals as the child involved wishes.

r little pig
ves me.
e with my pig
h me.

To my nephews, Justin, Benjamin, and Colby

—G.S.

To my good women friends

—C.H.

Oh, I love my little rooster
and my rooster loves me.

Oh, I love m
and my pig l
I'm gonna ri
as it rides wi

Little pig sings oink oink
Little rooster sings cockadoodle doo
a doodle doo a doodle doo.

Oh, I love my little chick chicks
and my chick chicks love me.
I'm gonna dance with my chick chicks
as they dance with me.

Little chicks sing peep peep
Little pig sings oink oink
Little rooster sings cockadoodle doo
    a doodle doo a doodle doo.

Oh, I love my little goose
and my goose loves me.

I'm gonna feed my little goose
as it feeds me.

Little goose sings honk honk
Little chicks sing peep peep
Little pig sings oink oink
Little rooster sings cockadoodle doo
    a doodle doo a doodle doo.

Oh, I love my little lamb
and my lamb loves me.

I'm gonna wash my little lamb
as it washes me.

Little lamb sings baa baa
Little goose sings honk honk
Little chicks sing peep peep

Little pig sings oink oink
Little rooster sings cockadoodle doo
a doodle doo a doodle doo.

Oh, I love my little baby
and my baby loves me.
I'm gonna read to my baby
as my baby reads to me.

Little baby sings la la
Little lamb sings baa baa
Little goose sings honk honk
Little chicks sing peep peep
Little pig sings oink oink
Little rooster sings cockadoodle doo—

and sweet dreams to you.